A Dolphin's Tale
A Whistle for Help

Written by Almaaz Gani
Inspired by a true story

Illustrated by Shayle Bester

AuthorHouse™ UK
1663 Liberty Drive
Bloomington, IN 47403 USA
www.authorhouse.co.uk
UK TFN: 0800 0148641 (Toll Free inside the UK)
UK Local: 02036 956322 (+44 20 3695 6322 from outside the UK)

Because of the dynamic nature of the Internet, any web addresses or links contained in this book may have changed since publication and may no longer be valid. The views expressed in this work are solely those of the author and do not necessarily reflect the views of the publisher, and the publisher hereby disclaims any responsibility for them.

Any people depicted in stock imagery provided by Getty Images are models, and such images are being used for illustrative purposes only. Certain stock imagery © Getty Images.

Interior Image Credit: Shayle Bester

This book is printed on acid-free paper.

ISBN: 979-8-8230-8309-6 (sc)
ISBN: 979-8-8230-8308-9 (e)

Print information available on the last page.

Published by AuthorHouse 06/23/2023

authorHOUSE®

Acknowledgments

I would like to thank my family for being my inspiration and my late grandfather Dr Khalid Ismail who taught me compassion, kindness and humility.

Thank you to my grandmother Khadija from Polokwane who has taught me to be brave despite the circumstances, and who has encouraged me to love books and nature, and who reminds me daily that learning is fun, no matter what your age.

Special thanks to the National Sea Rescue Institute of South Africa for inspiring me to get involved with wildlife conservation and for assisting me with photographs for my publication. Thank you to all those unnamed heroes and heroines out there who are involved selflessly in animal conservation. Together our conservation efforts can raise awareness on the importance of reducing and recycling plastic and the desperate need to find alternatives to make a change.

Almaaz Gani

For my grandfather
who was waiting for this

I wandered lonely as a Cloud
That floats on high o'er Vales and Hills,
When all at once I saw a crowd,
A host of golden Daffodils;
Beside the Lake, beneath the trees,
Fluttering and dancing in the breeze.

Continuous as the stars that shine
And twinkle on the Milky Way,
They stretched in never-ending line
Along the margin of a bay:
Ten thousand saw I at a glance,
Tossing their heads in sprightly dance.

The waves beside them danced, but they
Out-did the sparkling waves in glee:—
A Poet could not but be gay
In such a jocund company:
I gazed—and gazed—but little thought
What wealth the shew to me had brought:

For oft when on my couch I lie
In vacant or in pensive mood,
They flash upon that inward eye
Which is the bliss of solitude,
And then my heart with pleasure fills,
And dances with the Daffodils.
William Wordsworth

There is a delicate link that joins us all. Little Almaaz's story makes us aware that all life and living creatures matter. We can make a difference to the survival of all living species. Whether it be one thousand daffodils or a single dolphin, each has a unique and important role to play in our ecosystem. Each celebrates the beauty of nature and its purity. Nature has the power to uplift one's spirit and bring joy, even in moments of loneliness and solitude. Nature is a source of inspiration and happiness, and reminds us of the beauty and transience of life.

Khadija Ismail

"What humans do over the next 50 years will determine the fate of all life on the planet."

Sir David Attenborough

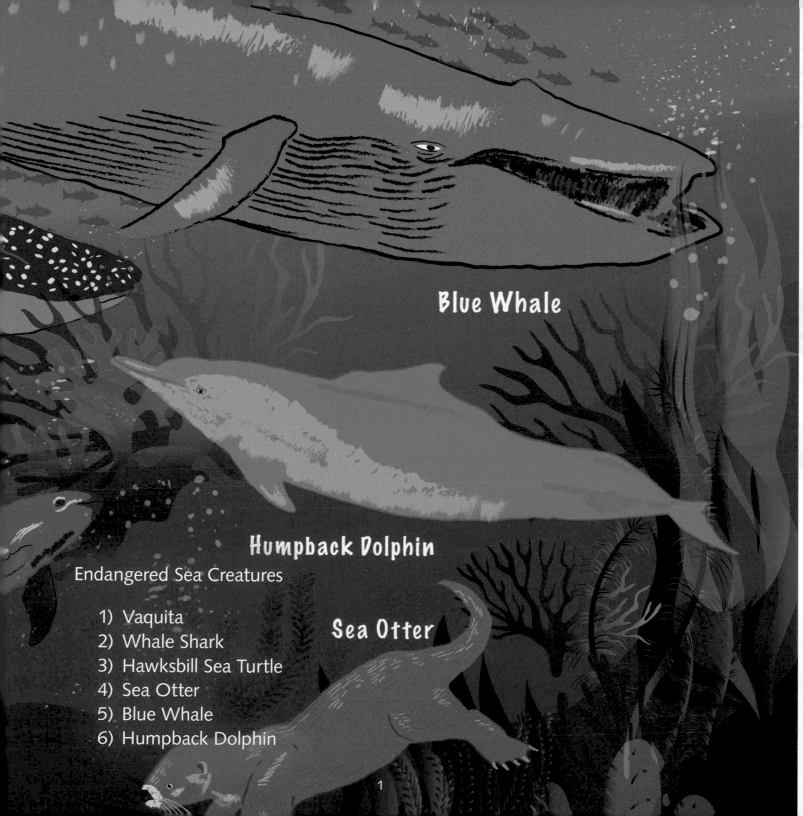

Blue Whale

Humpback Dolphin

Sea Otter

Endangered Sea Creatures

1) Vaquita
2) Whale Shark
3) Hawksbill Sea Turtle
4) Sea Otter
5) Blue Whale
6) Humpback Dolphin

Aqua watched as her siblings came back with their catches of fish.

She was the oldest in a family of bottlenose dolphins and they lived in the Pacific Ocean, between California and Hawaii.

Aqua was competing with her siblings for the privilege of being 'the best hunter'. She watched as the counts were displayed. Two, five, and seven. Easy!

4

She would always catch at least eight or nine at a time. "Watch this!" she said as she swam away for her turn.

The water blurred Aqua's vision as she chased after a school of fish, passing a breathtaking underwater landscape made up of vibrant corals and marine life. She let out a grunt of triumph as she caught eight with a single snap. This was too easy!

She celebrated as she rolled to her side playfully, breaching the water, swimming with one pectoral flipper raised high and slapping the water with her tail, creating a spectacular show.

Suddenly a broken piece of net with plastic debris came out of nowhere and caught Aqua's fin. She tried to get out of the net but as soon as she pushed out, water currents pushed her back down into the tangle.

She tried as hard as she could, but no matter how fast or hard she tried to swim out of the tangle, the current fought her back down.

Aqua had to think quickly. She could feel the force of the current sucking her further into the plastic debris. Fear gripped her. She kept her composure and looked around for an escape from the deadly, swirling water.

She reminded herself that she could swim, and she reassured herself that she could maneuver herself out of the plastic tangled net.

11

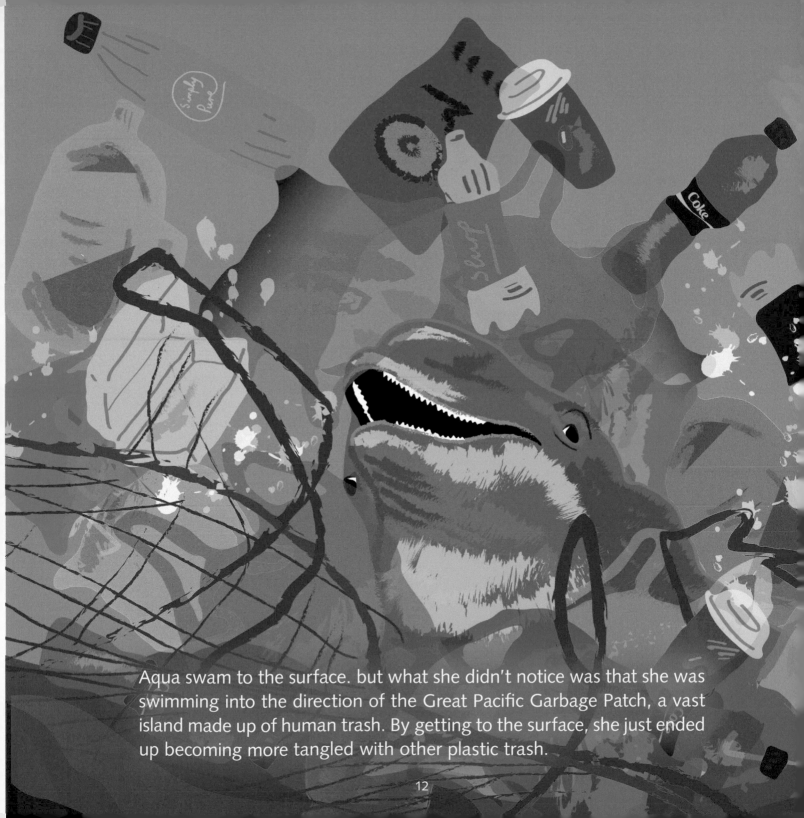

Aqua swam to the surface. but what she didn't notice was that she was swimming into the direction of the Great Pacific Garbage Patch, a vast island made up of human trash. By getting to the surface, she just ended up becoming more tangled with other plastic trash.

She felt all her triumph turn into fear when the air in her lungs began to disappear. Another net only tightened its hold on her neck, pulling her down, as she panicked and struggled.

Aqua tried calling out for help and her family, who were in the area, heard her calls.

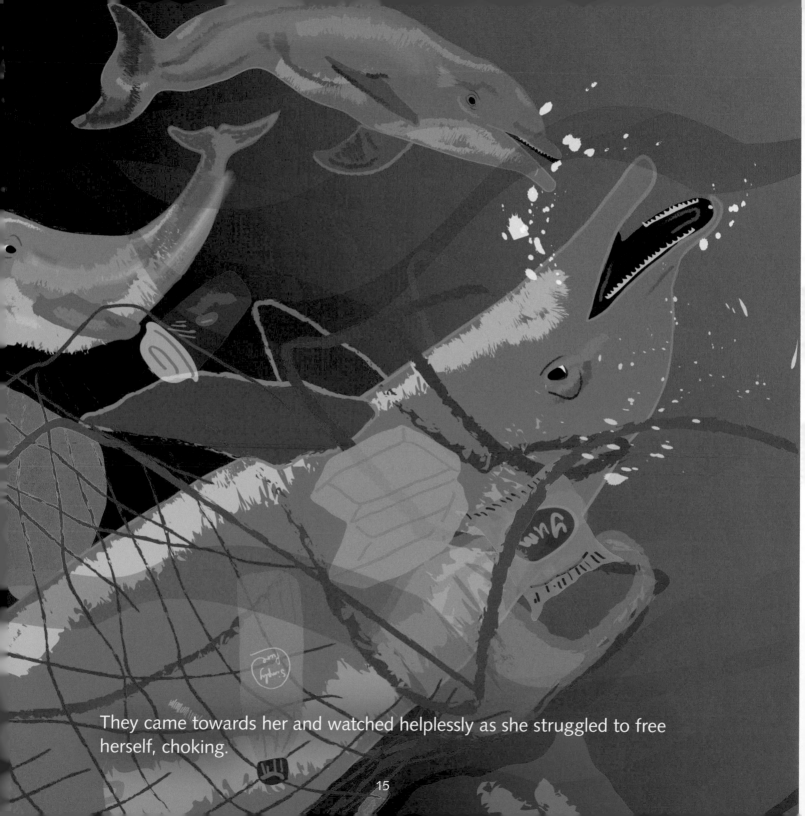

They came towards her and watched helplessly as she struggled to free herself, choking.

Just when all hope was lost, a miraculous Sea Rescue Boat appeared. The kind human beings helped to quickly untangle Aqua from all the plastic waste and she was rapidly released!

Aqua got lucky this time. What about the next?

Facts about dolphins

Even though dolphins live in the ocean, they are mammals, not fish. Like every mammal, dolphins are warm blooded. Unlike fish, who breathe through gills, dolphins breathe air using their lungs. Dolphins must make frequent trips to the surface of the water to catch a breath.

Other characteristics of dolphins that make them mammals rather than fish, are that they give birth to live young rather than laying eggs and they feed their young with milk. Dolphins, just like mammals, have a tiny amount of hair on their bodies. Dolphins produce a variety of vocalizations in the form of clicks and whistles. Dolphins have an excellent sense of hearing. They navigate their underwater world using echolocation.

Facts about dolphins

There are many different species of dolphins. Dolphins vary in size. They have streamlined bodies and two limbs that are modified into flippers. The average dolphin can swim up to 16 kilometres per hour and can leap up to 5 metres in the air. They leap clear of the water because air has less drag than water, hence saving them energy. They also chase alongside the bow waves of ships which helps them go fast using less energy.

Dolphins are often hunted, in an activity known as dolphin drive hunting. Besides drive hunting, they also face threats from bycatch, habitat loss, and marine pollution.

The effects of human activity on dolphins

Pollution is just one of the many human threats to dolphins. Marine animals face many different types of pollution. Chemical and oil pollution, plastic pollution and noise pollution are just a few of the many human-caused threats to dolphins.

Discarded plastic causes deaths in dolphins, whales and marine animals. Scientists estimate that approximately 56 percent of the world's dolphins and whales have ingested plastic at some point. The dolphins eat the plastic, misidentifying it as potential prey such as squid, and the plastic blocks their digestive system. Sharp-edged plastics also kill aquatic animals by punching holes in their internal organs.

The effects of human activity on dolphins

Plastic, that is found inside marine life, comes from plastic bags, bread tags, plastic bottles, bottle tops, straws and also synthetic fiber from clothing. Plastic is broken down into tiny plastic bits by the sun and waves. Dolphins also face entrapment and suffocation by discarded fishing gear, nets and plastic string. Human underwater sounds often cause dolphins to become disorientated, confused and in a state of panic.

Facts about the Great Pacific Garbage Patch

The situation of plastic pollution in the sea is so serious that there has been a huge accumulation of floating garbage in the Pacific Ocean, a real island composed mostly of plastic. The accumulation is thought to have started in the 1980's due to plastic pollution by man, and due to the rotating ocean currents in the North Pacific subtropical convergence zone. This huge island of garbage is known as the Pacific Ocean Trash Vortex or the Great Pacific Garbage Patch.

Its extent is not known precisely but it has been estimated to be more than 10 million square kilometers, an area that occupies a huge area of the Pacific Ocean. The amount of weight on this island is estimated to be millions of tons.

Like everything on Earth, this incredibly frightening garbage island is also home to life forms. It is possible to find about a thousand different types of heterotrophic, autotrophic, predatory and symbiont organisms, including diatoms and bacteria, some of which are seemingly capable of degrading plastics and hydrocarbons. On the surface, the island is home to numerous dangerous pathogens such as viruses and bacteria.

Special thanks to the National Sea Life Rescue Centre in South Africa

National Sea Life Rescue's partnership and association with conservation groups, animal sanctuaries and aquariums allow volunteers to track the progress of the animals rescued, especially the turtles, who often need lengthy rehabilitation.

Almaaz Gani encourages the youth to become involved with centres such as Sea Life Rescue Centre and to support organizations that help clean up pollutants and conserve wildlife.

She also encourages the youth to become involved in initiatives to recycle plastic bottles, bread tags, bottle tops and straws. You can also do your share by volunteering at beach clean-ups, eating sustainable seafood, using fertilizers and chemical pesticides appropriately. In this way, we will be able to minimize our carbon footprint and assist in the conservation of planet Earth for future generations.

All profits of this book will go to Wildlife
Conservation Centres in South Africa.

"The Ocean takes care of us,
let's return the favour."

Anon

"Eventually, we'll realize that if we destroy the ecosystem, we destroy ourselves."

Jonas Salk

About the author

Almaaz Gani is a budding 14 year old conservationist and lives in Polokwane, South Africa. She had envisioned this book with her grandfather when she was only 9 years old and stands today amongst South Africa's youngest authors. She lives with her parents Rehan and Kaamila and her siblings Ismail, Faizaan, Ameera and Omar. In her free time she loves to read and write, and spend time in her garden. She is currently schooling at Mitchell House where she has been encouraged and dared to be more (Nil Cedendum).

Her intention in publishing this book is to bring about awareness amongst the youth about conservation and the critical need for the youth to make a change.

Printed in the United States
by Baker & Taylor Publisher Services